T0132337

Adventures in Nite Lite Land

Michael Mattson

Copyright © 2019 Michael Mattson.

All rights reserved. No part of this book may be used or reproduced by any means, graphic, electronic, or mechanical, including photocopying, recording, taping or by any information storage retrieval system without the written permission of the author except in the case of brief quotations embodied in critical articles and reviews.

Balboa Press books may be ordered through booksellers or by contacting:

Balboa Press
A Division of Hay House
1663 Liberty Drive
Bloomington, IN 47403
www.balboapress.com
1 (877) 407-4847

Because of the dynamic nature of the Internet, any web addresses or links contained in this book may have changed since publication and may no longer be valid. The views expressed in this work are solely those of the author and do not necessarily reflect the views of the publisher, and the publisher hereby disclaims any responsibility for them.

Any people depicted in stock imagery provided by Getty Images are models, and such images are being used for illustrative purposes only. Certain stock imagery © Getty Images.

ISBN: 978-1-9822-3058-6 (sc)
ISBN: 978-1-9822-3059-3 (e)

Library of Congress Control Number: 2019908881

Print information available on the last page.

Balboa Press rev. date: 07/03/2019

BALBOA
PRESS

A DIVISION OF HAY HOUSE

Kyle's bedtime came just like every other day. His Mom and Dad kissed him good night and told him to have sweet dreams.

As he did every night when the bedroom light was turned off he looked at his night light and felt safe.

Then he closed his eyes for
another night's sleep.

Later that night he awoke to a sound. A small sound but a different sound. Not a creak of the house or the furnace starting up or any number of other noises you might hear in the night.

This was a small sound.
Then he heard it again,
and also saw movement
by his night light.

Slowly he got up from his bed and crept to the corner
of his room where the night light was plugged in.

Much to his surprise he saw a
group of very small people.

He slowly laid down on the floor in
front of them to get a better look.

One of the people stepped forward and
said, "Kyle we need your help."

Kyle asked how they knew his name. The little person replied that they knew all of the children's names at every house that had night lights.Kyle was amazed .He asked, "What can I do to help you?"

The small person said, "We have been watching you grow and realize that you are very brave and strong, and that you take very good of your sister."

Again Kyle was surprised at how much they knew about him and his family.

Kyle said, "You know my name, but what do they call you?"

The small person replied, "My name is Rudolfo. We live in a land inside your night light. We can come and go from your world to yours through any night light in the world. "

Kyle still didn't understand what he could do to help them.

Rudolfo said, "You must come with us to HELP STOP THE END OF OUR WORLD!"

Kyle said he would try to help.

Rudolfo gathered his people around Kyle. They began to chant.

Rink E Dink E Dinker De Do!

All of a sudden, Kyle felt himself shrinking. Everything around him was growing larger, his bed became huge. He had become the same size as Rudolfo. The night light began to glow brighter!

To go to Nite Lite Land,
Kyle must be small too!

The next thing he knew,
he was standing on a hill
overlooking a small village.
It was beautiful. The sky was
bright with millions of lights.

He commented on this to Rudolfo.
Rudolfo said each one of the lights in the
sky were night lights from somewhere
in Kyle's world. He explained that
in the morning when Kyle woke up
was when Rudolfo and his people
went to sleep because of the night
lights went out and it became dark.

During the day in Nite Lite Land was when they all went
about their business, growing crops, tending their animals
and the everyday business of life, just like back at home.

This is where they were in need of Kyle's help. A man named Bernard did not like to work and wished it was dark all the time. He had been going to children around the world trying to convince them they didn't need their night lights.

Little-by-little the sky was dimming, and slowly their days were getting a little darker. If this continued, the crops would no longer grow, then the people of Nite Lite Land would go hungry.

Kyle wondered to himself what he could possibly to do to help them. Kyle told Rudolfo he would need more help, and asked if he go back to his sister Kaelyn and his cousin Colton to help, too.

Rudolfo then gave Kyle a golden key. He said if Kyle kept it in his pocket, he could go into any night light in the whole world.

He went back to his own house through his night light. Once he returned to his normal size, he quickly went to Kaelyn's room to get her. He explained the whole story to a very groggy Kaelyn.

They walked over to Kaelyn's night light where Kyle repeated the chant. Then they both shrunk, and away they went! Before they knew it, they were in Colton's room. Kyle told Colton what was going on. He was excited to go with his cousins on this adventure.

All three held hands and repeated the chant.

"Rink E Dink E Dinker De Do! To go to Night Light Land, we must be small too!"

They shrunk down, the night light glowed bright, and the adventure began!

After reaching Nite Lite Land, Kyle said they needed to put their heads together to figure out a plan. Kaelyn thought they could go to all the children who turned their night lights off to explain what Bernard was doing, Colton thought that would take too long, so they all thought some more.

Finally, Kyle had an idea. Why not try to convince Bernard that working can be fun and that he could even enjoy it?

Colton said, "Good idea. Now we need to come up with a job that Bernard would like."

Kaelyn said, "I have it ! What job does every kid want to have?

Colton and Kyle looked at each other. They shrugged their shoulders confused…

Kaelyn exclaimed, "Bernard could drive an ice cream truck!"

So they went to Rudolfo and told him their plan. Rudolfo liked the idea. They had never had a truck to deliver ice cream in Nite Lite Land. But they did not have trucks in Nite Lite Land; they only rode bicycles, and used animals to pull their carts and wagons.

This was a problem until Colton suggested they put an insulated box on a bicycle to keep the ice cream cold.

They quickly got to work, finding supplies, and building the bike.

Later that day, Kyle rode out of Rudolfo'a barn on
a brand new ice cream bike for Bernard.

Rudolfo told them where Bernard lived and wished them luck.

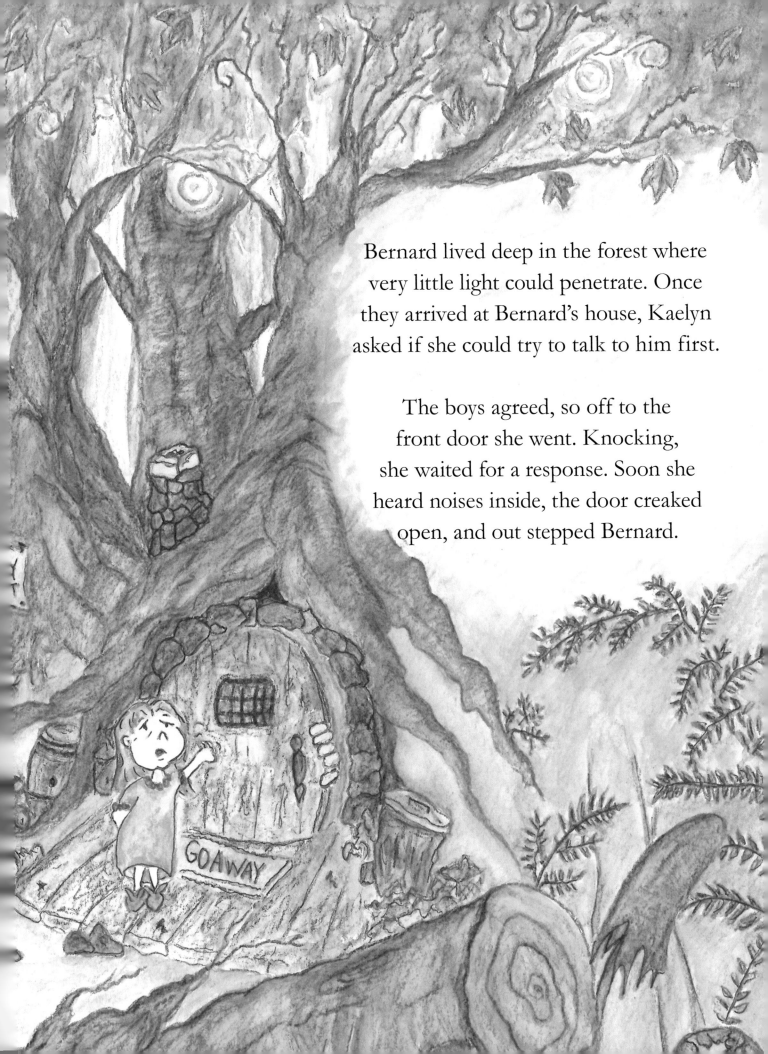

Bernard lived deep in the forest where very little light could penetrate. Once they arrived at Bernard's house, Kaelyn asked if she could try to talk to him first.

The boys agreed, so off to the front door she went. Knocking, she waited for a response. Soon she heard noises inside, the door creaked open, and out stepped Bernard.

GO AWAY

He was NOT happy that someone had disturbed his sleep. He asked Kaelyn what she wanted.

The little girl replied that she wanted to know why he wished to make Nite Lite Land dark. Bernard answered, "I don't like to work. If it was dark, I could sleep all day and all night."

Kaelyn asked, "When would you eat, or play with your friends or the animals?" Bernard said he didn't mind eating in the dark and that he and no friends or animals to play with.

She waved Kyle and Colton over, introduced them to
Bernard, and said that they could all be friends.

Bernard won't so sure.

Then Kyle brought the bike over. When they told Bernard
what it was for, a light flickered in his eyes.

He sat on the seat of the bike and smiled.
Then he looked at Colton and asked,
"But will people buy my ice cream?"

Colton replied, "OH YEAH!"

So off Bernard went house-to-house, ringing the bell on
his handle bars to announce his arrival. The children
ran out of their homes to see what was happening. They
were thrilled to see the ice cream on Bernard's bike.

Later that day, back at his home, Bernard showed Kyle, Colton, and Kaelyn his empty ice cream box and his full wallet.

With a huge smile on his face, Bernard said, "I never knew work could be so much fun. And I made a lot of new friends, too!"

Kaelyn asked, "So now will you stop putting out night lights?"

"Oh yes!" replied Bernard. "In fact, I will return to the children to convince them to turn their night lights back on."

Kyle, Kaelyn and Colton were so happy that they had been a part of Bernard's success. They said goodbye to Rudolfo and Bernard and the rest of their friends they had made and wished them all well.

Kyle tried to give the golden key back to Rudolfo. He wouldn't take it .He said "I hope that you and your family will come back to visit someday." Kyle assured him that they would take him up on his offer.

Returning home the three made a vow to keep the adventure to themselves. As they left Colton at his house and prepared to leave for home Kyle said, "If I've learned nothing else on this adventure. I've learned that having a family I can count on is more precious than any treasure in the world"!

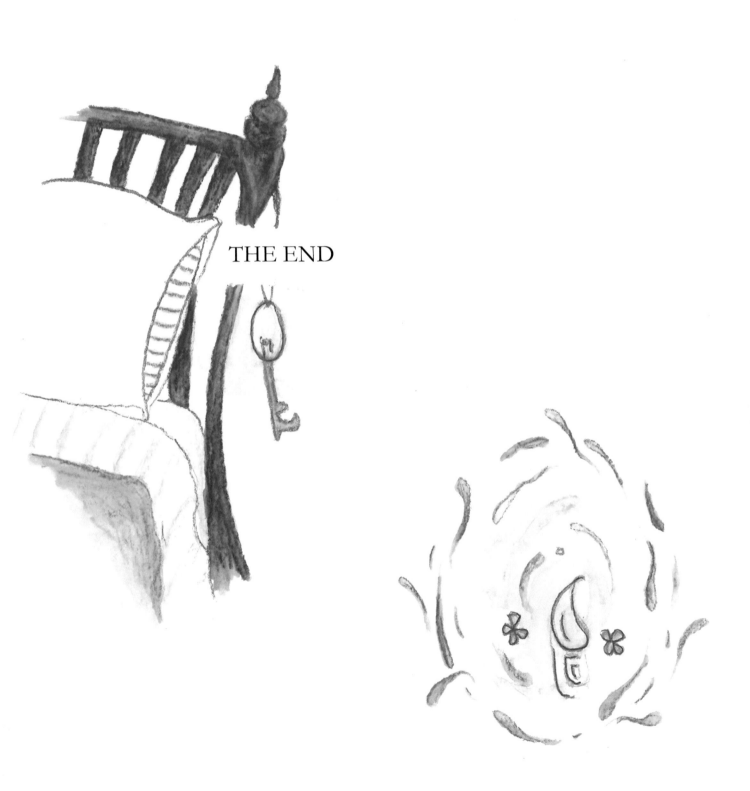

THE END

Printed in the United States
By Bookmasters